Usborne
Illustrated
Stories
from
Around
the
World

Edited by Lesley Sims
Designed by Caroline Spatz
Cover illustration by Laure Fournier

CONTENTS

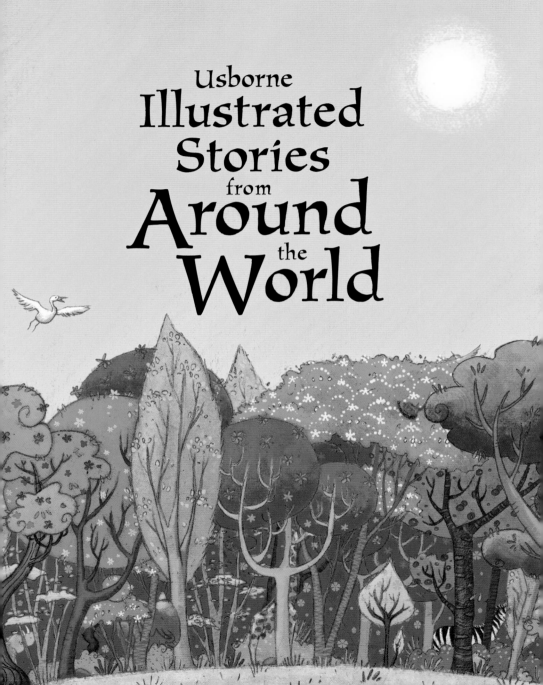

Usborne
Illustrated
Stories
from
Around
the
World

The
Baobab
Tree

A long,
long,
long,
time ago...

...the gods made the world.

They made the land and the sea. They made the animals and plants. One day, they even made a talking tree.

Hello!

At first, they were delighted with it. They watered it with showers of rain. They sent the sun to warm its leaves. And they called it the Baobab tree.

The Baobab tree talked and talked and talked. But it didn't talk about the gentle rain or the shining sun.

Instead, the Baobab tree moaned and groaned all day long – and all night too.

I don't like this soil.

When the weather was hot, the Baobab tree wasn't happy.

When the gods sent cool breezes, it complained about those.

The Baobab tree could always find something to be unhappy about.

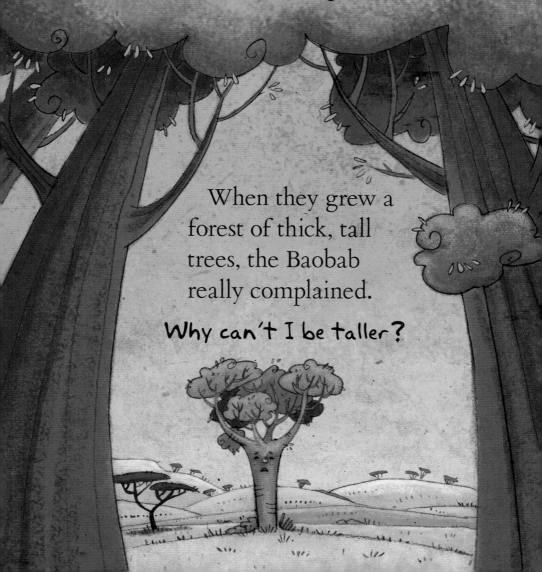

And it wouldn't let the gods get on with their work in peace.

When they grew a forest of thick, tall trees, the Baobab really complained.

Why can't I be taller?

"Not fair!" it whined. "I want to be taller. Make me taller."

The Baobab tree whinged and moaned so much, the gods were in despair.

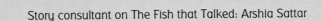

Story consultant on The Fish that Talked: Arshia Sattar

First published in 2010 by Usborne Publishing Ltd,
83-85 Saffron Hill, London EC1N 8RT, England.
www.usborne.com Copyright © 2010 Usborne Publishing Ltd.
The name Usborne and the devices 🎈 🎈 are Trade Marks of Usborne Publishing Ltd.

First published in America in 2010. UE.

The Fish that Talked comes from an ancient Indian poem called *The Mahabharata*. The original poem is 18 books long and over 2,000 years old. In some versions, it is the Hindu god Vishnu who takes the form of the fish.

King Midas was a king who lived in Ancient Greece around 3,000 years ago. According to legend, he washed off his golden touch in the river Pactolus. This river is in modern day Turkey. People still say that the stones on the river bed sparkle with gold.

Brer Rabbit Down the Well was written in the 19th century by Joel Chandler Harris, an American. He wrote a series of tales about Brer Rabbit but many of these stories are very similar to earlier African and Cherokee legends.

The Magic Pear Tree is a traditional Chinese folk tale. In some versions, the beggar is a Buddhist monk.

The Genie in the Bottle comes from a very old collection of stories known as *The Arabian Nights*. People say the stories were invented to entertain the King of Persia, by his beautiful and clever wife.

The Baobab tree didn't like those at all. "Why did you make me so plain and green?" it yelled up to the gods.

By now, the gods were furious. "We never should have made that tree," they muttered to themselves.

So they flew down to see the Baobab tree. "Stop moaning, or else," they warned.

Why should I? You can't make me!

The gods sighed and went back to
work, making wonderful fruit trees
that grew juicy, ripe fruit.

"I want fruit," bellowed the Baobab tree. "Can you hear me? I demand to have some fruit!"

"Stop!" cried the gods.

"We can't bear it any more. Stop talking!
We'll make you stop!"

They grabbed the Baobab tree and turned it upside down. Then they made a hole and thrust the tree into the ground... head first.

The Baobab tree was completely silent for the first time in its life.

The Baobab Tree

Its mouth was so
full of earth, it couldn't make a sound.

25

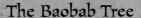

No one has ever heard the
Baobab tree say another word.

This is probably a good
thing for everyone.

Baba Yaga
the
Flying Witch

Baba Yaga the Flying Witch

Once upon a time, in a far off land...

...a little girl named Tasha lived with her father on the edge of a forest. Her mother had died when Tasha was very young.

Before she died, she gave her daughter a tiny doll. "Keep her safe in your pocket," she said. "There's no other doll like her in the world."

"If you are ever in danger, wait until you are alone, then give the doll food and water. She will help you."

A few years later, Tasha's father married again. "A new wife for me and a new mother for Tasha," he thought.

But his new wife had other ideas.

She waited until Tasha's father had to go on a long, long journey...

...then she called for Tasha.

Baba Yaga the Flying Witch

"I want you to go to Baba Yaga's hut in the forest," she cooed. "Ask her for a needle and thread."

Off you go!

But Baba Yaga is a witch!

Tasha sat on the doorstep and took her doll from her pocket.

She gave her a little piece of bread and a sip of water.

The little doll ate. The little doll drank. Then her eyes lit up like fireflies. Her arms moved... and so did her legs... She was alive!

"Little doll, little doll, help!" said Tasha. "Stepmother is sending me to the witch's hut. She gobbles up children as if they were chickens."

What shall I do?

"Do not fear," said the little doll. "I will protect you. I may be small, but I am powerful."

"Take some bread for Baba Yaga's dog and some ham for Baba Yaga's cat."

So Tasha packed the ham and bread
and set out through the deep, dark forest.

Soon, a wild wind began to blow.

Baba Yaga the Flying Witch

The trees creaked.
Their branches groaned.
Tasha looked up...

...and saw Baba Yaga zooming
through the forest in a flying pot.

41

She pushed herself along
with a wooden spoon.

And wiped away her tracks
with a long, wooden broom.

Tasha followed her to a strange little hut.
It twirled around on chicken's legs...

...and winked at Tasha
with its window-like eyes.

Baba Yaga stood in front of her hut and sang.

Magic hut, magic hut, turn around,
Bend your legs and touch the ground.

The magic hut spun on its bony legs and replied,

I can dance, I can see,
A little girl, in front of me.

"Ha-haa!" cried Baba Yaga, turning on Tasha. "What have we here?"

"P-p-please," said Tasha. "My stepmother sent me for a needle and thread."

Baba Yaga smiled a dreadful
smile. Her mouth was full of
iron teeth.

Her hair was greasy. Her hands were
warty. Her nose reached down past her chin.

"I can find you a needle and thread," croaked Baba Yaga. "But first you must sweep my hut."

She turned around and called for her maid. "Make me a nice big fire," she ordered. "I'm going to eat that little girl for lunch!"

She'll taste delicious!

But Tasha had overheard
Baba Yaga talking to her maid. Inside the
hut, she began to sob. "I don't want to be
eaten," she cried.

"Then give me that ham," said a skinny, black cat, "and I'll help you."

"Now, run away as fast as you can," purred the cat. "Baba Yaga will soon be after you in her flying pot."

But first, take these.

Thank you!

The cat pointed its paw to a golden comb and mirror lying on the floor. "When you hear Baba Yaga coming, throw down this magic mirror," it told her.

"If she keeps on coming, throw down the magic comb."

Tasha took the mirror and comb and ran outside...

...where Baba Yaga's big, black dog
was waiting.

It snarled. It growled. It ran up to Tasha
and showed its sharp teeth...

...and Tasha threw
it the bread.

The dog sniffed the
bread eagerly. "Keep
running!" it barked.
"Keep running!"

Back came Baba Yaga. "Are you sweeping, little girl?" she croaked, her belly rumbling with excitement.

"Yesssss, I'm sweeping," hissed the cat.

Baba Yaga leaped into her hut. "Where's the girl?" she screamed at her cat.

Why did you help her?

"I've served you for a long time," said the cat. "But you've never given me food. That girl gave me ham to eat."

In a fury, Baba Yaga raced out to her dog.

"You let her go! Why didn't you stop her?" she shouted.

"I've served you for a long time," said the dog. "But you've never given me food. That girl gave me bread to eat."

Baba Yaga gnashed her iron teeth.

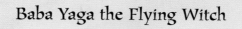

She didn't wait a moment longer,
but jumped into her pot.

She pushed off with
her wooden spoon.

60

And she zoomed into the air, sweeping away her tracks with her long, wooden broom.

Thump! Thump! Thump! went the spoon. **Swish! Swish! Swish!** went the broom.

"Baba Yaga's coming," cried the little doll.

Tasha threw down
the mirror.

It touched the ground
and exploded into a wide,
rushing river.

63

"Curses!" cried Baba Yaga. She bent her bony body and drank...
and drank...
and drank...

She gurgled and guzzled until
there wasn't a drop of water left.

Then, once again, Tasha heard the **thumping** spoon and the **swishing** broom.

"Baba Yaga's coming," cried the little doll. So Tasha threw down the comb.

66

A huge mountain
sprang up behind her.

"Curses!" cried Baba Yaga,
and she began to chew through
the mountain.

67

But her iron teeth were rusty from drinking the wide, rushing river.

One by one, her iron teeth snapped.

"Curses!" cried Baba Yaga.
"I'll have to go back. No little
girls for lunch today."

With a **thump! thump! thump!**
and a **swish! swish! swish!**
Baba Yaga sped back to her magic hut.

Tasha didn't stop running until she reached home.

Her father rushed out to meet her. "Where have you been?" he asked.

"Stepmother sent me to Baba Yaga's hut," gasped Tasha. "And the witch tried to eat me."

71

"Then it's time your stepmother left," said her father.

And he threw her out of the house.

She was never seen again.

74

The Stonecutter

The Stonecutter

Once upon a time, there lived a humble stonecutter.

He worked hard but he also grumbled –
all day long.

I'm tired.

I need a
break.

This stone is
too hard.

The Stonecutter

A passing mountain spirit heard
him complain and stopped to listen.

Agh!
My back aches.

Ouch!
My arm hurts!

"Poor man, he
sounds so unhappy,"
thought the
mountain spirit.

A few days later, a wealthy merchant visited the stonecutter. "I'm building a new wall in my garden," he said. "I'll take one hundred of your finest blocks."

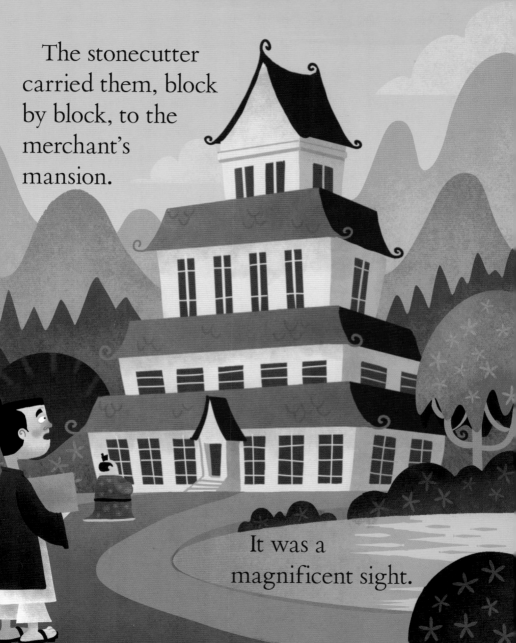

The stonecutter
carried them, block
by block, to the
merchant's
mansion.

It was a
magnificent sight.

"Wow!" said the stonecutter. "If only *I* were rich..."

The Stonecutter

Up on a cloud, the mountain spirit heard his wish. The old spirit smiled and raised his hand...

...and, in the blink of an eye, the stonecutter *was* rich.

Now he had a magnificent house too.
And he didn't need to work. He could sit in
his garden all day long, instead.

But still he wasn't happy.
"It's too hot out here with the sun
beating down on me..." He paused.
"I think *I'd* like to be the sun!"

The Stonecutter

The mountain spirit heard him. He raised his hand...

...and, in a shower of sparks, the stonecutter *was* the sun.

Flowers bloomed, children
played and everyone was happy
– even the stonecutter.

87

But soon he was
grumbling again
– and so was
everyone else.

As he shone down, the flowers
turned brown and the rivers dried up.

The Stonecutter

"This is no fun," said the stonecutter sun.

Just then, a cloud
began to rain.

Everyone cheered.
"I'm fed up being the sun.
I think I'd like to be a cloud," said
the stonecutter.

The mountain spirit smiled once more. (He was a very patient soul.) He waved his hand...

...and the stonecutter was a cloud.

The stonecutter rained... and rained. The problem was, he couldn't stop raining.

Rivers overflowed and flooded the land.

Soon, water covered everything except the mountains.

"I wish *I* were a mountain," sighed the stonecutter.

The mountain spirit smiled again...

The stonecutter liked being a mountain. He liked the breeze ruffling through his grass hair, and birds singing to him from a tree on the top of his head.

At last, he was happy. Then another stonecutter began to cut chunks off him.

The Stonecutter

"Hey! Stop that! OUCH!" he cried. But the other stonecutter didn't hear him. "I don't want to be a mountain anymore," he said. "I wish I were a stonecutter."

The mountain spirit smiled one last time.

He raised both hands and, in an explosion of stars, the stonecutter was back where he started.

98

Dick Whittington

There was once a boy named Dick Whittington, who lived in the English countryside. Dick was very, very poor.

He had no money to mend his shoes when they wore out.

He could never find much to eat.

He didn't even have a home to take shelter when it rained.

"I need a job," he thought.

So Dick looked for work.
He asked boatmen...

builders...

...and
blacksmiths.

But no one he met on his
travels needed any help.

102

Dick had heard of London.
It was a big city, many miles away.

"I've never been there myself,"
said the farmer. "But they say the
streets are paved with gold."

104

"Gold!" thought Dick. "I could make my fortune. Then I'll buy fancy clothes, piles of yummy food and a big house."

He thanked the farmer and set off.

Dick walked for miles...

LONDON
50 miles

and miles...

LONDON
25 miles

...and miles.

LONDON
10 miles

But when he arrived in London, he got a shock.

The streets weren't made of gold at all. "They're just plain old dirty stone," said Dick, sadly.

Dick had no choice but to look for work once more. He asked bakers...

butchers...

...and boot menders.

But it was the same story as before. No one needed his help.

Soon it started to get dark, so Dick searched for somewhere to spend the night.

Yawn! This will have to do.

He curled up on the steps of a grand-looking house. It wasn't long before he was fast asleep.

109

The next morning, Dick was woken by the sound of a very loud voice, bellowing in his ear.

Get off my lovely clean steps!

A woman was standing over him, waving a rolling pin. "Get out of here!" she yelled.

Dick had never been in such a fine
house before. It was full of the
most beautiful things he'd
ever seen.

Wow!

"Welcome to my home," said the man. "My name is Mr. Fitzwarren and I'm a trader. My ships buy and sell things all over the world."

He showed Dick a chair from France, a vase from China, a statue from Africa and a big wooden chest all the way from India.

After Mr. Fitzwarren had heard Dick's story, he felt sorry for the young boy. So he gave him a job in his kitchen.

Dick spent the day washing pots...

cleaning floors...

...and peeling carrots.

It was long, hard work.

But Dick was happy with his new life.
And all the other servants in the house
were kind to him.

Good job, Dick!

Well done, lad.

Well, almost all...

Out of my way, scruffpot!

After his first day's work, one of the kitchen maids showed Dick to the attic at the very top of the house. He'd never had a room of his own before.

Hooray! A proper bed at last.

The attic was small, but Dick didn't mind. He climbed into bed and snuggled under a big, warm blanket.

But just as he began to fall asleep, he heard a loud **squeak!** It was coming from down below.

Dick peered over the edge of the bed.
Suddenly, a mouse squeezed out of a hole
in the floorboards...

Squeak!

followed by
another...

Squeak!

Squeak!

...and another.

Soon the attic was full of noisy mice.

Dick couldn't get
a wink of sleep.

120

It was the same thing every night. At first, all was quiet. But just as Dick's tired head hit the pillow...

...the mice came out of their hidey-holes.

The annoying mice were driving Dick crazy. "I must get rid of them," he thought. "Or I'll never get to sleep again."

A week later, Mr. Fitzwarren gave Dick his first ever pay.

"Here you are," he said, handing Dick a shiny coin.

Wow! A whole penny.

Dick couldn't wait to go out and spend his hard-earned money.

That afternoon, Dick visited the city market. There were hundreds of stalls, all packed with goodies.

Ye cream cakes
5 pennies each

Ye bread rolls
4 for a penny

Ye rhubarb sticks
1 penny a bag

Dick Whittington

Ye bramble smoothies
1 penny each

Ye personal music player
1 penny

Then, on the far side of the market, he spotted just the thing he needed.

☙ YE PETS ☙

Puppies
2 pennies
each

Grow your own
frogs
1 penny per jar

Cats
1 penny each

"A cat will keep those noisy mice away," thought Dick, taking out his penny.

He handed over his week's wages to the stall holder. Then he chose the biggest cat from the basket and ran home.

I'll call you Tom.

"We'll show those pesky mice," said Dick, stroking his new friend.

That night, the mice appeared as usual. But, this time, Dick was ready for them.

Go get them, Tom!

Tom darted around the room and chased the mice back into their holes.

Dick breathed a sigh of relief. "At last, I can get a good night's rest," he thought to himself.

Dick and Tom curled up together and were soon sound asleep.

The next day, Mr. Fitzwarren gathered the servants together in his study. Dick wondered what he was going to say.

"One of my ships is going on a trading trip," announced Mr. Fitzwarren.

"If you have anything you want to sell, it can go on the ship. She sails at six o'clock tonight."

Dick thought for a moment.

He only had one thing to sell – his cat. Maybe he wouldn't need Tom now all the mice were gone.

"Perhaps someone will give me two pennies for him," thought Dick.

He put Tom onto the cart that was going to Mr. Fitzwarren's ship. But, as it drove away, Dick began to wonder if he'd done the right thing.

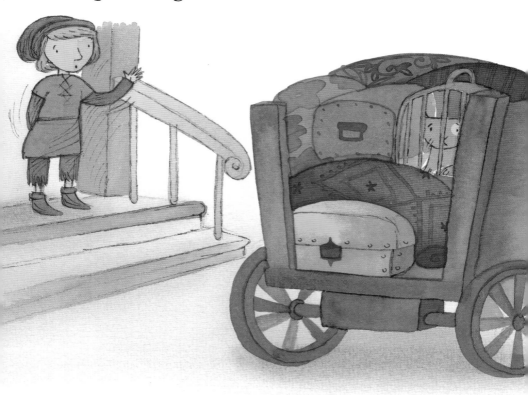

That night, Dick couldn't sleep.

He felt bad about selling Tom. And now the mice were back too.

Squeak!

Squeak!

The next day, Dick wandered around the house in a sleepy daze.

"Wake up, you lazy boy!" growled Mrs. Curry, the cook. "Work harder, or I'll report you to Mr. Fitzwarren."

From then on, Mrs. Curry made Dick work twice as hard as anyone else.

After a month of Mrs. Curry's nagging, Dick was fed up.

"I'm going back to the countryside," he thought to himself.

So, early one morning, he slipped quietly out of the house before anyone else was awake.

He walked and walked, until he reached the outskirts of London. Just then, the church bells rang out.

"That's strange," thought Dick, pricking up his ears. "The bells sound like they're calling to me."

Turn again Whittington, thrice mayor of London.

Dick was amazed. "They seem to be telling me to go back..."

"...and they're saying I'll be the mayor of London – three times. How odd."

Dick could hardly believe his ears.
But he went back to Mr. Fitzwarren's
house all the same.

When he got there, he found
Mr. Fitzwarren waiting for him
on the doorstep.

"Congratulations, Dick," boomed Mr. Fitzwarren, holding up two bulging bags. "You're a very rich young man!"

Rich? Me? How?

"The king of Barbary bought your cat," explained Mr. Fitzwarren.

"His palace was full of mice," continued Dick's old boss. "Tom chased them off."

Mr. Fitzwarren handed Dick the two bags. When he opened them, Dick found they were stuffed full of shiny gold coins. "They're all yours!" said Mr. Fitzwarren.

Dick used the money to buy and sell things, just like Mr. Fitzwarren. He was a big success.

By the time he had grown up, Dick was one of the richest men in the city.

What's more, the bells were right. Dick did become the mayor of London three times – and he was the best one ever.

146

The Three Wishes

The Three Wishes

Ned and Nat were so poor, they never had enough to eat. "I'm hungry," Ned grumbled, rubbing his stomach.

Nat sighed. "Well, that was the last of the cabbage," she said. "There's no food left."

149

Ned went to his job in the fields, his stomach rumbling. He was cutting some hay when he heard a tiny cry.

Please help me - I'm stuck!

To his astonishment, he saw a fairy
– trapped in the hay and panicking. He
gently unhooked her wing from a haystalk
and smiled.

"Thank you! Thank you! Please let me grant you three wishes," said the fairy.

Ned's smile grew bigger. "Three wishes, eh?" he thought.

The Three Wishes

Hardly able to
believe his luck,
Ned ran home to
tell Nat the amazing news.

The Three Wishes

"Nat! Nat! I rescued a fairy.
We have three wishes!"
he shouted.

Inside their cottage, Nat looked thoughtful. "Three whole wishes," she said. "Just think what we could wish. Ooh, I wish for..."

"A sausage!" said Ned.
There was a ting! And a sausage
appeared on a plate.

"A sausage?" screeched Nat. "Of all the foolish, ridiculous, thoughtless, stupid, ludicrous, idiotic and downright silly things to wish for."

You fool!

Now, Ned was cross. How dare Nat speak to him like that?

"There's nothing wrong with wishing for a sausage," he said. "And such a fine one too. I think you need to take a closer look at it. I wish it was on the end of your nose!"

Ting!

The Three Wishes

And it was.

Nat was livid. Even Ned looked
shocked. "Don't just stand there.
GET IT OFF!" demanded
Nat. But the sausage
would not budge.

The Three Wishes

"Oops!" said Ned.

"Oops?" screamed Nat. "Oops? Is that all you have to say?"

"Sorry?" Ned tried.

"Ned," wailed Nat. "I can't go around with a sausage on the end of my nose.
Do something!"

Ned sighed. "I wish the sausage was off your nose," he said.

Ting!

And it was.

Nat stroked her sausage-free nose
in relief.

"Now we have no wishes left,"
Nat said, sadly.

"No... but we do have
a sausage!" said Ned,
with a grin.

The
Fish
that
Talked

Long ago, in India, there lived a young man named Manu. He was kind and good, and loved by all the animals.

One day, Manu was wading in a
cool, clear stream when suddenly...

...a shining fish
swam into his hands.

The Fish that Talked

The fish sparkled with a strange, silvery light. Manu lifted his hands to take a closer look.

The Fish that Talked

To his astonishment, the fish spoke.
"Help!" it begged. "The big fish
are trying to eat me."

The Fish that Talked

Manu was astounded. He'd never even heard of a talking fish. The fish gave a shiver. "You poor thing," said Manu, gazing down at the tiny, terrified creature.

He couldn't put it back
with the big fish. So, holding
it in his cupped hands, he
carefully carried it home.

179

There, he dropped the talking fish into a
jar of water...

Splash!

...and fed it with crumbs.

At once, the
fish began
to grow.

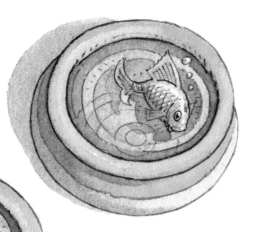

It grew and
grew...

I have
no room to
swim.

...until it was too big for the jar.

So Manu took the fish outside
to the well, and fed it with bread.

Splash!

Again, it grew and grew...

I have
no room to
play.

...until, very soon, it was
too big for the well.

The Fish that Talked

So Manu carried the
fish to the river.

This time, he didn't
feed it but...

185

...it still grew and grew and grew.
Manu couldn't believe his eyes.

there must be something
fishy going on!

Now the fish was
ENORMOUS.

187

The Fish that Talked

The fish was too big even for the river.
"Please take me to the sea," it begged.

Manu groaned. "He'll weigh a ton,"
he thought. But aloud, he said, "I'll try."

And amazingly, despite its huge size,
the fish felt as light as air.

189

The Fish that Talked

Manu carried the fish to the seashore.
He clambered over rocks, to the edge of
the deep water. Then he threw the fish
into the foaming waves.

191

Before it swam away, the fish looked at Manu and smiled.

"Thank you," it said. "You are a good man. Now it's my turn to help you."

"There is going to be a great flood."

"You must build a boat to save all living things. The future depends on you."

193

The Fish that Talked

So Manu built a huge,
wooden boat.

194

He filled it with plants and animals
- from tiny ants to enormous elephants.

Soon, dark clouds filled the sky.
Lightning flashed...

...and rain came lashing down.

It rained and rained, until water covered
all the land, as far as anyone could see.

198

Only Manu's boat floated above the waves, full of braying, honking animals.

Then the wind whipped up and huge waves crashed around the boat.

Manu bit his lip. "We must find shelter," he realized, "or we'll sink!"

He frowned into the darkness – and saw
a strange, silvery light. His frown faded.

The Fish that Talked

The talking fish was back! "I've come to help you," it called. "Throw me a rope."

The fish pulled the boat through the storm. After many, many days, they reached a great mountain.

Its top rose out of
the flood like an island.
  "We'll be safe now," sighed Manu.

205

Suddenly, the fish changed.

Then it spoke. "I am Brahma, lord of all creatures," it said.

Manu gasped and gave a deep bow.
Brahma was a powerful god.

207

"I have saved you so you can rebuild the world," said Brahma.

"And you, Manu,
will be its king."

"Rule wisely!" said Brahma
sternly, looking Manu
straight in the eye.

"I will," promised Manu.

Brahma vanished in a flash of silvery light.

Manu never saw Brahma or the
talking fish again. But he never forgot
what the god had told him.

After the flood, he worked hard to rebuild the world.

And he ruled wisely and well for the rest of his days.

King Midas
and the
Golden Touch

King Midas was a very rich
man. He may have been the
richest man in the world.

He had so much money, he would stroll around town, throwing gold coins to the people he passed.

One day, as he was walking through the palace gardens, he met an old man.

"I came out for a walk," said the old man, "and now I'm completely lost. Please can you help me?"

King Midas took his arm and they walked along every street, until at last they found his home. The old man's son was very relieved to see them.

"Meet my son," the old man said to King Midas, introducing them. "He's a powerful god, you know."

"I want to thank you for helping me and my son has agreed to grant you a wish. Name whatever you want."

King Midas thought for
a moment. "What do I really,
really want? Well, I do love gold..."

"I know!" he said. "I wish I had a magic touch. Whenever I touch something, I want it to turn into gold!"

"If you're sure..." said the god. "It's yours!"

King Midas bent down to pick up his wooden walking stick...

Immediately, it turned to solid gold.

King Midas rushed straight back to his palace. He touched the old stone pillars...

With a shimmer, they were gold too.
King Midas was delighted.

He decided to have a feast to celebrate
and he invited the old man and his son
to join him. But the
second he touched
the food...

...it turned to gold. He almost broke his tooth on a golden chicken leg.

"I'm hungry!" wailed King Midas, beckoning a servant. "Sorry," he added, as the servant turned to gold. "Please make it stop," he begged the god.

"I'm afraid there's only one way," said the god. "You must travel for seven days, over the mountains and beyond a great forest, to a magical river."

"Find the river and bathe yourself in it.
Your golden touch will be washed away.
You'd better take your golden servant, too!"

Midas set out, followed by an exhausted
servant who was dragging his
golden friend.

After journeying for seven days, they found the magic river. King Midas reached down to touch the soothing water. It didn't turn to gold.

He jumped in...

...and the water washed away his golden touch. His servant was cured and even his stick was wood once more. King Midas spluttered with relief. "I see you can have too much of anything – even gold," he said.

Brer Rabbit
Down the Well

There once was a cunning young rabbit, named Brer Rabbit.

Brer Rabbit's worst enemy was Brer Fox. They were always playing tricks on each other.

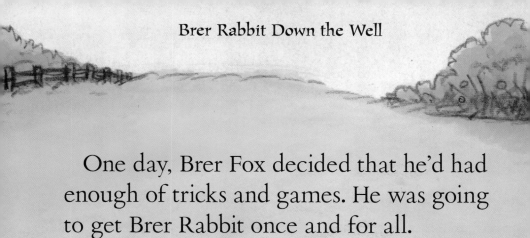

One day, Brer Fox decided that he'd had enough of tricks and games. He was going to get Brer Rabbit once and for all.

He chased Brer Rabbit through the fields.
"I'm going to eat you up," he growled.

Brer Rabbit ran as fast as he could, but
Brer Fox was close behind.

I need a clever
plan – now!

At last, Brer Rabbit
came to a deep, dark
well. He stopped
and looked inside.

"I'll hide in here,"
he thought. It wasn't that clever
a plan, but it would do for now.

He jumped into the bucket at the top of the well. As he hopped in, the bucket rocked.

The handle of the well began to spin – faster and faster. The bucket began to fall. Brer Rabbit screamed. "AGHHHH!"

The
bucket
fell...

AGHHHH!

...and
fell...

AGHHHH!

...and fell!

Splosh!

The bucket landed with a splosh at the bottom of the well. "However will I get out?" Brer Rabbit thought.

"I heard you screaming," called a voice from the top of the well. "Ha! I've got you now."

Brer Rabbit saw Brer Fox's pointed snout and two greedy eyes peering down at him.

"Why did you think that was a good place to hide?" asked Brer Fox. "You're more stupid than I thought."

"Oh no, I'm not. I'd never be so stupid as to hide in a well that I couldn't get out of," said Brer Rabbit. "You see, I'm not hiding at all."

"I'm fishing!"

"There are some huge, juicy fish down here."

Splash!

He made a splashing sound with his paw as if he were grabbing a big, fat fish from the water.

"I've got one," cried Brer Rabbit. "It's the biggest fish I've ever seen. I think it weighs more than I do."

He splashed his foot. "Wow! Now I've caught two big, fat fish."

Splash!

"You should really come down here yourself," he added. "Or there won't be any left for you."

255

Now, Brer Fox loved eating fish. In fact, he loved fish even more than he hated Brer Rabbit. His mouth began to water.

"I can take all of Brer Rabbit's catch too," he thought. "Oh, I can almost taste those juicy, fat fish already."

He turned the handle on the well as
quickly as he could. The bucket came up.

Brer Rabbit hopped out and Brer Fox
climbed in. He didn't stop to wonder why
Brer Rabbit wasn't carrying any fish.

Then Brer
Fox fell...

...and
fell...

...and
fell.

Splash!

The well was cold and dark and clammy. His whiskers and his tail were dripping wet. "This better be worth it," he snarled.

Brer Rabbit just laughed.

Brer Fox looked around and splashed in the water with his paw.

"Where are the fish?" he growled.

"In the river," said
Brer Rabbit. "Where
they usually are."

"In fact, all this excitement has made me
hungry. I think I'll go and catch some
right now."

Brer Fox howled with anger. "Noooooo! You tricked me! You tricked me!"

But Brer Rabbit wasn't
listening. He was strolling away
in the direction of the river and
whistling a cheerful tune.

HELP!

It took Brer Fox a *very, very*
long time to climb out of that
deep, dark well.

265

The Magic Pear Tree

Selfish Shen lived all by himself, in a little house with a big garden.

The Magic Pear Tree

In the middle of his garden grew
a tree. One summer, it was covered
in sweet, golden pears.

269

There were far too many for Shen. But he couldn't bear the thought of sharing them with anyone else.

Instead, he picked every single pear and packed them into a box. "I'll sell them at the market," he chuckled greedily.

They should fetch a pretty penny!

The Magic Pear Tree

Shen set his box of pears on a table and called out to the people browsing in the market.

Pears for sale!

A beggar stopped to admire the plump, golden fruit. "Please could I have one?" he asked.

Shen looked at the beggar's rags and frowned. "Can you pay?" he snapped.

"No," said the beggar sadly, holding up empty hands. "I don't have any money."

"Then go away and stop bothering me!" shouted Shen.

A kind woman overheard Shen shouting.

She tapped Shen on the shoulder. "Couldn't you spare just *one* pear?" she said gently.

"After all," she went on, "the poor man must be hungry and you have more than enough to share."

"NO!" yelled Shen selfishly. And he glared at her over the pears.

Shen expected the woman to give up and go away. But instead, she pulled out her purse and bought a pear...

...and gave it to the beggar herself.

"Thank you," said the beggar gratefully. "That was very kind of you."

281

The beggar gazed hungrily at the pear for a moment. Then he gobbled it up, stalk and all.

In a few gulps, it was gone. A moment later, he spat out a handful of little black seeds.

"Mmm, delicious," sighed the beggar,
licking the last of the juice from his lips.

He turned to the woman. "Now, it's my turn to give *you* a pear."

"Aha!" cried Shen. "So you DO have money! You were just pretending to be poor, to try and trick me."

But the beggar shook his head. "No," he said, looking Shen straight in the eye. "Truly, I haven't got a penny."

The woman was puzzled. "If you have no money, how will you get another pear?" she asked.

The beggar smiled. "I'll show you," he said. "Just watch this..."

A crowd of curious passers-by joined
Shen and the woman to watch.

The beggar dug a little hole and dropped in the handful of seeds. He whispered some magic words...

Then he glanced up. "Please could I have some hot water?" he asked.

A tea-seller brought over a pot of
steaming tea. "Will this do?" he asked.
"Perfect," cried the beggar.

Carefully, the beggar poured hot tea into the hole. Steam billowed up, hiding everything for a moment.

When it cleared, the crowd gasped.
Something was shooting up out of the hole
– something with twigs and leaves.

It must
be magic!

The something grew and grew.

It grew into a magnificent
tree, with gleaming leaves
and golden pears.

297

When the tree had stopped growing,
the beggar picked a pear and handed it
to the woman.

"Mmm, delicious," she exclaimed,
between sweet, juicy mouthfuls.

299

The beggar turned to the crowd. "Who else would like a pear?"

"Me! Me! Me!" they shouted, reaching
out eager hands.

The beggar picked pear after golden pear, handing them out to the crowd, until the tree was bare.

Everyone got one – even selfish Shen. It was the best pear he had ever tasted.

Mmm, delicious!

Now everyone was busy eating, no one
was watching the beggar.

Quickly, quietly, he chopped down the tree and strolled away.

Oh no!

When Shen finished his pear, he glanced around – and gasped in shock. He could not believe his eyes.

All of his precious pears had gone! And their wooden box was chopped to pieces. "Wh-wh-what?" he stuttered. "H-how?"

All too late, he realized. "We've been tricked," he yelled. "Those pears the beggar picked – they were mine!"

"The beggar turned my box into a tree by magic, so he could steal my pears."

That mean old thief!

Shen was absolutely furious at the
beggar's trick. He was left with nothing
but a red face. The crowd just laughed.

"You deserved it," they told him. "Now perhaps you'll be less selfish next time."

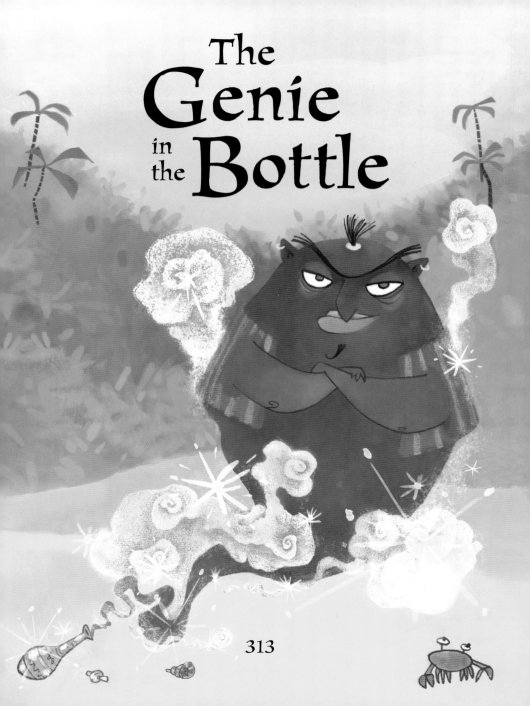

The Genie in the Bottle

313

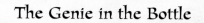

The Genie in the Bottle

Once upon a time, a poor
fisherman went down to the sea.

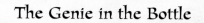

He threw his net again and again,
hoping to catch a fish for his supper.

He caught plenty of
slimy seaweed...

...a few shiny shells...

Yuck!

...and even a smelly old sock – but he didn't catch one fish.

Then, he felt
something heavy.
"A fish!" he thought
eagerly. He hauled up
the net...

The Genie in the Bottle

...and peered at his catch in surprise.
It wasn't a fish at all. It was an old bottle.

Curious, he pulled out the stopper and
looked in – but he couldn't see anything.

320

"Empty," he sighed sadly, throwing the bottle away.

CLUNK!

But he was wrong...

The bottle bounced twice and smoke
began billowing out. The smoke formed
into a big, bad, angry face.

"Help," cried the fisherman, as smoke coiled around him and his cat. "It's a bad genie!"

The big, bad genie's
tummy rumbled.

"I'm hungry," he growled. He stared at the fisherman and licked his lips. "I need to eat something. I think I'll start with YOU!"

Meow!

"That's not very nice," said the fisherman bravely. "After all, I'm the one who set you free."

I don't care.

"I don't want to be nice," boomed
the genie. "I'm starving! I've been in
that bottle with nothing to eat for a
hundred years."

The fisherman thought fast. He knew that, somehow, he had to get the genie back in the bottle. Luckily, he had an idea...

"You were really *inside* this bottle?" he asked.

"YES," snapped the genie impatiently.

"A great big genie like you, inside this little bottle?" teased the fisherman. "I don't believe it. You'd never fit!"

"Watch," said the genie crossly.

Whoosh

He whooshed back in...

...and, in a flash, the fisherman jammed in the stopper.

Whew!

Grrrrr

Then the fisherman went on fishing.
This time, he had better luck.

Purrrr

That night, the fisherman and his cat feasted on tasty fish – with not a genie in sight.

About the stories

The Baobab Tree is based on a South African tale. The baobab tree is a real tree that looks as if its roots are in the air, so people came up with stories to explain its strange shape.

Baba Yaga is a famous witch-like character who appears in the folk tales of Russia and many Eastern European countries.

The Stonecutter is a traditional tale from Japan, but similar stories are told across Europe. These feature different unhappy characters, including a woman who lives in a vinegar bottle.

Dick (Richard) Whittington was a real person who lived in England from about 1350 to 1423. He grew up in Gloucestershire and went to London to find work. He became a successful cloth merchant and was mayor of London three times.

The Three Wishes is an old folk tale from Northern Europe. The version in this collection is adapted from the tale told in Sweden.

Still, they got on with their job. Next,
they made all kinds of pretty trees. Some
had soft pink blossoms.
Others had bright
red flowers.